For Y

The
the Brunette &
the
VENGEFUL
Redhead

Robert Hewett

lotsa
Dave xxx

Currency Press, Sydney

First published in 2007
by Currency Press Pty Ltd,
PO Box 2287, Strawberry Hills, NSW, 2012, Australia
enquiries@currency.com.au
www.currency.com.au

Copyright © Robert Hewett, 2007.

NATIONAL LIBRARY OF AUSTRALIA CIP DATA

Hewett, Robert, 1949–
The blonde, the brunette and the vengeful redhead.
ISBN 9780868198064.
1. Man-woman relationships – Drama.
2. Interpersonal relations – Drama. I. Title.
A822.3

Set by Dean Nottle for Currency Press.
Cover design by Kate Florance, Currency Press.
Printed by Hyde Park Press, Richmond, SA.

The Blonde, the Brunette and the Vengeful Redhead
was first produced by Stewart D'Arrietta for
Saxophone Productions at the Stables Theatre,
Sydney, on 26 February 2004 with the following
participants:

Performer	Jacki Weaver
Director	Jennifer Hagan
Assistant Director	Sean Taylor
Designer	Laurence Eastwood
Lighting Designer	Peter Neufeld
Sound Designer	Wei Han Liao
Composer	Stewart D'Arrietta

COPYING FOR EDUCATIONAL PURPOSES
The Australian Copyright Act 1968 (Act) allows a
maximum of one chapter or 10% of this book, whichever
is the greater, to be copied by any educational institution
for its educational purposes provided that that
educational institution (or the body that administers it)
has given a remuneration notice to Copyright Agency
Limited (CAL) under the Act.
For details of the CAL licence for educational institutions
contact CAL, 19/157 Liverpool Street, Sydney, NSW, 2000.
Tel: (02) 9394 7600; Fax: (02) 9394 7601;
E-mail: info@copyright.com.au.

COPYING FOR OTHER PURPOSES
Except as permitted under the Act, for example a fair
dealing for the purposes of study, research, criticism or
review, no part of this book may be reproduced, stored in
a retrieval system, or transmitted in any form or by any
means without prior written permission. All enquiries
should be made to the publisher at the address above.

Any performance or public reading of *The Blonde, the
Brunette and the Vengeful Redhead* is forbidden unless
a licence has been received from the author or the
author's agent. The purchase of this book in no way
gives the purchaser the right to perform the plays in
public, whether by means of a staged production or a
reading. All applications for public performance should be
addressed to Currency Press.

The actress, the director and the balding writer

This story began with an almighty whinge. If it had been measured like an earthquake, it would have shot right off the Richter scale. It came in the form of an e-mail from an actress. Part of it read: '… and I've just won Best Actress, Best Director, been awarded a Lifetime Achievement Award and I'm broke and out of work!' It has always been thus.

We are old friends and a whinge via email, phone or in person is allowed.

I'd been having a bit of a lazy time (I can quite happily sit staring out the window for hours, with nothing of note going on between my two ears), but this e-mail galvanized me into action. The plan: to write a play my friend could produce and perform, then tuck away in her bag, ready to be pulled out whenever the coffers were getting a bit low.

I finished what I call a 'splat down'—a rough draft that literally goes splat down on the page. Who cares about spelling and punctuation? You can fix all that later. The main point is that it has a beginning and gets to an end. I shot this off to my friend. She liked what she read, making a suggestion or two which I incorporated into the next draft. With text, production budget and application forms in hand, my friend now set about applying to the various funding bodies in her state. If they were keen, she would be up and running; if not, well… there the story would have ended.

In the meantime, in another part of Australia, another old friend was having lunch with director Jennifer Hagan, who inquired what I was up to. Namely, did I have any two-handers lying about in my bottom drawer? Jacki Weaver, a well-known Australian actress had recently married and was keen to do a play with her new husband. I didn't have a two-hander, but there was *The Blonde*, as the text had now been christened. It was sent off, with the proviso that certain territories were already spoken for, but if Jacki was interested, she could have the rest of Oz. They both responded positively.

So now Jacki began trying to haul in a budget. Not an easy thing to do. Then came bad news. My friend, for whom I had written the play, had been turned down by the funding bodies. A bitter disappointment. Graciously, she wrote to me and said to give her rights to Jacki.

This was November. By December we had a producer, designer, lighting designer and a theatre booked. A definite opening night loomed, but no money, with rehearsals due to begin in three weeks. Things fell off the rails a little until, finally, the money was in place.

At this stage I hadn't actually had a face-to-face with anyone. I was in Melbourne, they were in

Sydney; everything had been done by phone and e-mail. Our first meeting was a January 'workshop'—four days put aside to work through the play, page by page.

We were in high-humidity Sydney, rehearsing in a borrowed flat in Randwick, directly opposite the racetrack. Me on the floor, having grabbed the only coffee table to lay out the text; the Assistant Director in the one armchair; the Director sitting erect on a lone kitchen chair; and Jacki standing beside a wardrobe rack of clothing. Ah, the glamour of showbiz!

Jacki didn't do a read-through, but proceeded to do a run of the play, partial costume changes and all. For the next four days we went through the text, breaking it down scene by scene, character by character. I went home to my sister's family at night, booting my nephews out of their bedroom while I hit the computer, so by the end of the four days I could leave the crew with the next working draft. This was a good time. Nothing about the story had changed, but perceptions had. Decisions were made, ideas enriched—a consolidating time for all.

Rehearsals proper began two weeks later. I was in Melbourne 800 kilometers away, so all requests for further re-writes came in via e-mail after rehearsal. I'd work on them that night and send them back, usually in time for the following day. It wasn't until the last week that I went back up to Sydney. This time, when I arrived at the space, a kindergarten hall in the inner Sydney suburb of Newtown, very serious discussions were being held by mature adults sitting on chairs designed for midgets.

Backsides very near the ground, knees around the ears, there was no room for airs or graces here. There were problems; they were sorted.

A run-through, a pack-up and move to the theatre, a preview, then an opening. This was February. It had only been five months. The Blonde, the Director, and the Balding Writer had done it. We opened to a wonderful reaction from both audience and critics.

Slightly stunned I retreated back to my home in Melbourne. By the second week the tiny Stables Theatre in Sydney was selling out and there were waiting lists for tickets. Interest from the major companies followed. The production and play began to receive international attention, and within months there were offers from various countries.

With each new country it was decided to place the play in the context of that society. The story remains exactly the same, as do the characters and their actions. However, localising the piece brings immediacy to the events, recognition and identification for the audience. Very little change to the text occurs.

In Toronto recently, for the North American premiere of the Canadian production, I went in search of some fruit. It was a Saturday afternoon, and there was a game on. I was repeatedly asked for, or offered tickets for 'the game', but no one was able to help me in my quest for some fresh fruit. In the end, and not knowing the area at all, I just followed the crowds. Finally I hit pay dirt. The crowd had lead me into a large multi-storied shopping mall.

Looking around I could have been in Melbourne, I could have been in Manchester, but I was in Toronto, thousands of miles from either of those places.

The only thing that was different were the accents and the local coffee franchise.

Enjoy the play.

Robert Hewett

Character and setting

All characters are played by the one actor.

The following was my original idea for the setting:
  Three panels spread across the stage.
  Each panel has a central pivot, so that it can be manipulated independently or in unison with the others if desired. The central panel is set back so that the three form a triangle.
  Each panel can be lit so it appears either transparent or solid as required.
  At the end of each scene the panels close to conceal the actress as she enters the central area.
  The panels are lit at this time to allow the audience to view the transformation in silouette.
  The panels then open to reveal the new character and the action continues.
  However, for the original production, the setting consisted of a single clothes line, hung with washing, in the centre of which was a large sheet. Images denoting each locale were projected onto this.
  A red garden seat, centre stage. At one side of the stage, a dressing table with mirror, costume, and wig stands.
  Whilst the actress was changing so would the projected images, until the next locale was established, and the action continued. All costume changes occurred onstage in view of the audience.

Subsequent productions have had an opaque plexiglass screen, backlit, where the actress can change, seen in silhouette, with images projected above until the next locale is established and the actress steps out to reveal the next character.

Bottom line—keep it simple.

The published text is of the original Australian production. Subsequent productions have been localised. For example, the Australian 'mate' becomes 'pal' or 'buddy' in the US and Canada; 'Perc Hennessy's sub-newsagency' becomes 'Perc Hennessy's dairy' in New Zealand, 'variety store' or 'corner store' in the US and Canada; the term 'bloody' becomes 'goddamn' in the US and Canada; and so forth. It gives the text immediacy for the audience, and once the actress speaks in her own accent, the context is set. Apart from Mrs Carlisle, isolated in what was once a working-class suburb now undergoing gentrification, we are in middle-class suburbia.

ACT ONE

Rhonda's story

The mournful sound of a woman keening.
A door slams shut.
Rhonda Russell enters. Over forty, red hair, wearing a raincoat.
She frantically searches her pockets, but comes up empty-handed.
She searches her handbag and pulls out several items, before replacing them, not having found what she's looking for.

Rhonda What is happening?

You weren't going to say anything, Rhonda.

You weren't even going to go there!

Think, Rhonda, think.

Was it Lynette's idea?

Lynette's been the best neighbour a girl could want. Especially in times of crisis. A real 'friend indeed'. So how… how?!

   Rhonda addresses the audience.

You see, it was Lynette who saw them this afternoon. Down at North Course Plaza.

Outside McDonald's. I mean, Graham rarely eats McDonald's. The only time in living memory that I can remember Graham eating fast food was after we'd been to Bob and Gay Thornycroft's re-affirmation of their wedding vows.

The food at Bob and Gay's was so bloody awful, Graham made me pull over on the way home and he threw up out the car window.

Then he asked me to pull into a McDonald's so he could line his stomach before heading to footy practice.

Graham loves his footy. He's the oldest member of the team. Some weekends he spends more time on the bench than on the field.

But he usually gets a kick in the last ten minutes. Especially if they're losing by a big margin. No harm done then. And he does love it.

Anyway, my neighbour Lynette saw Graham, and this blonde, down at North Course Plaza this afternoon.

I mean, he moved out two months ago. Got a flat.

Graham wouldn't tell me where. Hardly said a word, really. When I sit down and think about it, which I do, often, well to be honest, I find no real reason for the breakdown of our marriage.

The whole episode's been a bit surreal. That's how I'd sum it up, anyway. No real screaming match. Nothing like that. Not really Graham's style. He just shuts up. You know, closes off.

When Graham's in a mood like that it's like trying to have a conversation with a block of wood.

'How was work today, Graham?'

'All right.'

And that's all I get out of him for the next fifteen minutes.

Well, this night he walks in the door and I say, 'Hello, Graham'.

No verbal response, just a nod.

'You want to go over to Lynette and Dennis's tonight?'

'Why?'

That's all. Not hello, how's your father, nothing but 'why?'

And Graham's walking out the kitchen door, down the hall, out of sight into our bedroom.

Well, the phone rings, doesn't it?

Lynette, of course. On the phone quicker than Flash Gordon.

She's seen Graham's car pull into the driveway and wants to know if we're coming over after dinner.

And I lie, and say, 'Be there straight after, don't go to any trouble though, Lynette'.

I hate lying to a friend like that.

Anyway, one morning I get this phone call from Graham.

He's at work, and he says he's moved out.

Moved out?

I mean, when someone, when your husband, in this case Graham, my partner who's been living under the same roof for the past seventeen and half years, says something like that to you, well, you don't necessarily jump straight in with the right questions.

Well, not me anyway.

Am I stupid or something? I don't believe I am.

I was in IT before I met Graham.

On the ground floor in Research and Development.

Had quite a few colleagues in Silicone Valley.

Oh yes, I had those opportunities, but when you marry, you have to make choices.

And for me, having a family was utmost.

Our first and our second pregnancies… well, I lost both.

And then we had Damien.

Life-changing event. Wonderful.

Made everything worthwhile.

Once Damien was at school, I tried to get back in, but technology was so advanced… The dogs may still be barking, but the caravan had moved on. Well and truly.

Originally, I was very successful in IT, perhaps not so good at marriage.

You see, I thought Graham meant he'd moved out. You know, into another office at work.

Not moved out of our home.

That concept just didn't connect. Not in this head.

But that, in fact, is just what he was talking about.

Graham was talking about our home.

Our marriage. My life.

Him and me.

Graham Russell and Rhonda Russell.

And Graham Russell was telling Rhonda Russell, me, that he'd moved out of my life.

That is how my brain began to compute the information.

In blocks.

Until I finally put all the blocks together and the picture became clear.

'Out where, for God's sake?'

Graham didn't have anywhere to move out to.

You do need a little more than your briefcase and your lunch to move into a place by yourself.

But it was in that instant, the microchips were working a little faster now, that another thought occurred to me.

Perhaps, just perhaps, it might be that... that, I'd almost successfully blocked the thought, but it was now oozing—well gushing, really—through the cracks in the old brain.

Perhaps Graham wasn't moving into a place by himself.

Whoawh!

Hold your horses!

All right, Rhonda. Allow your grey matter time to compute.

Step back.

Acknowledge, but don't necessarily accept.

This is dangerous territory.

Wheels are already in motion.

That's what this phone call is about.

Think, Rhonda, think!

I'm flying blind in my own kitchen!

Think, brain! Help me, for God's sake!

Graham's leaving, or rather has left our home. And he isn't necessarily moving into a place by himself!

Right. This, of course, was hindsight.

I was still coming to terms with the first words he'd uttered.

'I'm moving out.'

It's not the sort of phone call I'd ever had at nine-forty on a Wednesday morning. I was barely in the back door, from dropping Damien at school, picking up some dry-cleaning and getting some worming tablets for the cat. That's where my head was at.

What's more, I ducked into a No Parking spot outside the vet's, because there's never a park, and got a bloody ticket!

Bastard.

So I've just walked in the door—parking ticket, dry-cleaning and worming tablets—and the phone rings and it's Graham.

And my life has changed irrevocably.

> *Rhonda bends her head, covers her face with her hands. She fights back tears. She pulls a handkerchief from her sleeve, goes to wipe her nose, then sees that the handkerchief is covered in blood. She screws it up in her hand and conceals it in her pocket.*

You know what I did after I hung up?

I moved about our house, almost as if I was not inside my body. I watched myself ever so calmly hang the dry-cleaning in the wardrobe.

Opened Graham's side to see, yes, there did seem to be odd bits and pieces missing. Could be in the washing basket? Not to worry.

So I closed the wardrobe door and watched myself walk down the hall and into the kitchen.

The cat was there. Mr James, our old tom.

And I put my black bag down on the kitchen table and took out the worming tablets.

'Gosh these are big tablets.' And I start to read the instructions, look at the cat, and really have to think hard.

Do I absolutely have to give the cat its worming tablets now?

Should I wait 'til later?

Why not pop over and see... who? Who should I tell first?

You see, I've always told Graham everything first.

He's always the first one I tell anything to.

But not this.

And the cat starts rubbing up against my leg.

Well, I pick up the phone and... I ring Graham at work.

It's the most natural thing in the world to do.

Pick up the phone and ring your husband at work.

And Graham answers.

And I say, 'You just rang me...'

I didn't say hello or anything.

Well, you don't. Not after seventeen and a half years.

It's a matrimonial shorthand. It's woven into our lives.

And I say, 'Have you left me?'

And Graham doesn't say anything,

'Graham, help me… help me, please. I need to comprehend this. Have you just left me?'

And still there is nothing.

He hadn't hung up. I could still hear his breathing.

'Graham, you said you'd pick up Damien from the Hudsons' tonight. Lynette's picking them up from school, then dropping the boys off for Tim's birthday. Can you still pick them up afterwards?'

I'd let him off the hook. Just like that.

I'd deflected. Given him an out.

But still there was nothing!

'Graham, I just need to know if you can pick up Damien after Tim Hudson's birthday party tonight like we arranged!'

Still nothing.

'If this isn't possible, I'll have to make alternative arrangements. Can you pick them up?'

'No, I can't. You'll have to make alternative arrangements.'

That blunt.

That ungiving.

'Graham, answer me! Have you left me?!'

'I already told you that.'

He put me on the back foot. Just like that.

I was asking a dumb question, the answer to which he'd already told me, and which I already knew, and I was making him tell me again.

But I couldn't stop myself.

'Yes, I know you've already told me. But why?'

The phone went dead.

He'd hung up on me. That's when the poor cat copped it.

I mean, I didn't aim the worming tablets at Mr James, but the bottle exploded somewhere near his backside and he shot out the door.

Closely followed by me.

Went straight over to Lynette's, completely forgetting she works two days a week at North Course Plaza and wouldn't be home 'til at least four.

Of course. I'd just discussed the arrangements with Graham.

Lynette's doing the pick-up from school, dropping Damien off at Tim Hudson's birthday party.

What now? Where to now?

I leapt into the car and shot off to school, then thought better of it and headed to Lynette's work.

You know, I must have walked past Donovan's Discount Jewellery hundreds of times. Meeting Lynette for coffee. Picking up something for

Damien from Kmart. Never in my wildest dreams imagining that it would figure so prominently in my life.

That's where she worked. The blonde.

Donovan's Discount Jewellery.

Not that I knew it then. I was still completely in the dark as to whether there was another woman or not? Was this a mid-life crisis on Graham's part? Knew nothing then.

Well, I grab the first park I can at North Course. Stride through the mall, up the escalators. Past Kmart, past Wendy's, past Muffin Break and straight into Lynette's shop.

Lynette drops everything when she sees me.

I'd kept it together 'til then.

But the look on her face, I don't know what I looked like, but hers was a big smile that suddenly vanished.

'Hi, Rhonda. What are you doing here?'

At that precise second, the floodgates opened.

I couldn't help myself, and I couldn't stop the tears.

They were streaming down my face.

Well, Lynette slams a whole lot of bras she's holding down on the counter, brushes aside a mother and daughter she's serving, and wheels me into a change room.

'Be with you in a moment, madam.'

Don't know how many hours I was there.

Lynette keeps ducking in and out.

Tissues, coffee, more tissues, more coffee, until I realised that I must have been in that little change room for over two and a half hours. Don't know how any of the women tried on bras?

With Lynette's help I somehow pull myself together enough to get through the rest of the day.

And the next one, and then following week, and then fortnight, and then month and then...

'Rhonda! I've seen them.'

It's Lynette. This afternoon, a few hours ago.

Crashing through the side gate, straight down the hallway into my bathroom. I'm sitting on the loo, of course.

'Rhonda, I've seen them!'

'Who?'

'Who do you think? Them!'

'Them who?'

Lynette thrusts out her hand, flushes the toilet and spits out the word one more time.

'Them!'

'Oh.'

That one word confirmed... everything.

12

It was true.

I'd completely denied the possibility.

Denied that there could be anyone else involved.

This was something between Graham and myself. To be sorted out only by Graham and myself.

Another woman? Never. I'd wiped that possibility right off the list.

'And you'll never guess where she works?'

'Where?'

I was pulling up my knickers, zipping up my slacks.

'Down the escalators from me at the discount jewellery place. Donovan's. Rhonda, you've got to confront her.'

The words seemed so innocent. Almost practical.

'Confront her?'

As I said it wasn't my idea, it was Lynette's.

'Confront her? Oh, I couldn't do that.'

I was trying to wash my hands, but Lynette grabs me, looks me straight in the eye and says, 'You have to, Rhonda. You have to do this for the last seventeen years of your life or what has it all meant?'

Well, that hit home.

'You have to do this, Rhonda, for the sake of your marriage. For your child's sake. But most importantly, you have to do this for you. Confront her.'

So I did.

I confronted the blonde.

Rhonda takes out the bloodstained handkerchief, unravels it, then holds it up to the light.

I've never been in a police station before tonight.

Never.

She folds the handkerchief.

The keening sound builds as the lights fade.

This is drowned by the sound of an approaching police siren which, in turn, is swallowed by the trucks, vans and machines of an industrial suburb.

Doctor Alex Doucette's story

Alex You get all sorts in this practice. It's a clear geographical division. There's the old boys from the Salvation Army home up the road. That's to the north. There's the lovelies from the drug rehab centre, that's due south. They're possibly our most fabulous clients. Usually reed-thin. Swear black and blue they aren't being serviced by the rehab centre. I mean, we've had prescription pads stolen, then re-presented at the dispensary here, with my forged signature. Now, presenting a prescription to where they actually stole it from, then putting my name on it, a doctor who actually works there? It's real rocket science.

I get buzzed by our pharmacist. 'Got another one.' I dutifully trot down.

Examine the script. Smile up at the client, and politely explain, 'Well, actually I'm Doctor Alex Doucette and that's not my signature'.

To which the usual response is: 'Big fuckin' smart-arse, aren't you?'

And that is due south.

Now due west, we have the Housing Commission.

And due east, well that's the escape route.

Across the river is 'El Dorado'. That's where we all want to head. Set up practice.

I've always been committed to social causes. It's a real joke amongst my friends.

'Dr Doucette. The Dyke Who Has To Do. Do Everybloodything.' But I do really believe social and economic inequality is unacceptable in this country. We are, after all, a wealthy society. And the divide between the haves and have nots is growing wider by the minute. You look around here where my clinic is, and it's crap.

You look across the river, that's where I came from, it might as well be another planet.

I've been fortunate. And it's only by accident of birth. Born in England, into an adoring family, surrounded by love.

Even in my difficult adolescent years my parents were angels. Believe me, I was a difficult bitch. My coming-out, unlike a lot of my girlfriends, was a piece of cake.

Add to that the normal middle-class privileges. Mum and Dad could afford private education, university, et cetera, et cetera. I'm not putting myself or my achievements down.

Yes, I have the brains. Yes, I have the application. More importantly, it's also been ingrained in me from childhood, I must give back.

My partner Chrissie thinks I give too much back.

Striking the balance can be hard, and with a lot of the extreme cases that we get in here, it's rarely, if ever, a black and white issue. Only have to work in a practice like this for a week to have your social outlook dramatically redefined.

And Chrissie's right.

You can give and give and give 'til there's nothing left for you. That's dumb.

Took me a few years to learn that one. And you've got to keep some of yourself for the most precious person in your life, my partner Christine.

And my mum and dad, too. I owe them so much.

But if you're going to get involved with someone like me, then you have to be understanding too.

If I'm dealing with someone in crisis, I can't just say, 'Time's up'.

For Chrissie I know how frustrating it is if I walk in the door an hour, two hours late.

I understand, the grief reception are getting if there's a waiting room full of clients, we're running forty-five minutes behind, and there's a client, like this chap I saw yesterday, came in for a script of anti-depressants.

And you ask, 'Why?'

Normal procedural questioning.

But that triggers a flood.

Whoosh. Out it all comes.

Crap he's been bottling up for years.

I'm a GP, for chrisake!

But I can't boot him out. He's a middle-aged man. And he's bawling his eyes out in front of his quack he's only seen twice in the last two years for a flu shot.

And suddenly this businessman's crying his eyes out saying he's left his wife of so many years and he's fallen for another woman, and he wants anti-depressants.

'No worries, mate, here's your script, off you go.'

If only.

No, he's confused. His work's suffering, and he's moved out of the family home months ago. But now he's missing his child desperately, but if he goes back it'll give false hope to his wife.

He's in love with some chick who runs a chain of jewellery stores. And he's obsessed with her.

But she's not so sure.

She's got this bloke well and truly by the balls.

He's sobbing. And I can see the time ticking over. And Despina our receptionist comes over the intercom, 'Excuse me, Alex, but six patients waiting. And there's an urgent message to ring Chris.'

And then my client gets all apologetic, wants to wrap it up.

Like it's some business deal. Snap. Sign here. Deal done.

I can't send him off half-baked. First duty is to the patient, but he's already closed shop for the day, so I have to find a way back in.

I recommend a psych.

He won't have a bar of it. Deal's off.

I try to reinforce. 'It's not a weakness, it's a sign of strength. You accept you need help.'

He still won't buy it.

I say, 'Don't dismiss the concept, give it time, think it over'.

And Despina's buzzing on the intercom. There's an urgent call from St Vincent's, can I take it? So I tell her to find out the details, I'll call them back.

In the meantime, my client is just about backing out the door apologising for his behaviour, he's been under a lot of stress, et cetera, et cetera. You just want to scream at the jerk: 'But that's why you came here, and you won't accept my help'. But he takes his script and goes.

And that's when Despina says I have to take Chrissie's call.

'It's St Vincent's Hospital on the line.'

I don't know what Despina's talking about.

'Despina, is it St Vincent's, or Chrissie?'

'No, Chrissie's been admitted to St Vincent's.'

> *Dr Doucette takes her stethoscope from her neck and wraps it around her hand. It gives her time to pull herself together.*

Music is heard.

Images from a cat scan of the brain appear.

Clinically speaking.

A hairline fracture of the skull is not fatal. And a hairline fracture is what I'd been told to expect.

But by the time I get to St V's, this 'hairline fracture' is a 'multiple fracture', and there's a real possibility of internal bleeding. The brain's taken a severe blow, and there's pressure in the frontal lobe area.

I'm halfway through discussing options with the chief registrar when Sam and the kids come into view.

Little Matthew and Ellen.

What's he bringing them here for?

Sam and I haven't always been on the most harmonious of terms. But just lately things have settled down. A bit.

Sam is Ellen's father after all, Chrissie's her mother. Sam was Chrissie's husband.

Me?

Well, I was the 'Wicked Pommie Bitch of the West' who'd swept in on her broomstick and whipped gorgeous wife Chrissie from his loving arms. Truth be known, the marriage was long dead before I ever appeared on the scene.

Ellen had proved a difficult child. As Ellen grew, her problems became more traumatic. Special needs. Special schools.

Sam and Chrissie had both had affairs. Sam was spending the odd weekend with, can't remember her name. Not important now.

If the marriage wasn't on the rocks, it was definitely smashing up against them well before I ever appeared.

And I was a threat to Sam's masculinity.

Sam had been passed over for another woman? Quelle horror.

But as I said, things aren't too bad of late.

His and Chrissie's marriage is almost ancient history. The divorce was six years ago, and Christmas is complicated, but manageable.

Chrissie and I have our own son Matthew.

I don't stay over at Chrissie's every night. I've got my own place near the clinic.

And even though Matthew has a habit of calling Sam 'Dad' because Ellen does, Sam is not, I repeat not, the biological father.

It sometimes gets to me, Matthew calling Sam 'Dad'.

But those things you can sort out later on.

We are a family. In our eyes, anyway.

What I don't understand is why this had to happen? Why to us?

Is it just fate? Is it your turn? What?

What has Christine ever done to deserve this?

Some half-crazed idiot attacking her.

There's my partner lying comatose on the other side of the door in St V's. This gentle creature I kissed goodbye just a few hours before, fighting for her life.

The registrar, a lovely man called Reg Collins, is telling me the best neuro's on his way over, but we are going to have to make a decision, quick smart.

Based on what they could see so far, if the brain continues to swell, there is a possibility of seizure, or fitting.

That's when I look up and see Sam heading down the corridor with Matthew and Ellen.

And Reg keeps talking. He thinks we might have to remove the front section of the skull. It's the latest procedure. This relieves pressure, allows the brain to swell, replace that section with a plastic composite.

Suddenly… Sam is at my elbow, with Matthew and Ellen.

Sam… puts his arm around my shoulder.

Well, I lose it.

'Life and death options? What the fuck has this to do with my life?!'

I push my way into the ward. Reg follows. Sam wisely keeps Ellen and Matthew out in the corridor.

Chrissie's lying unconscious. Her head is being cropped of all hair, and a young male nurse is shaving the stubble.

But there is a large patch of scalp where her hair's already missing.

An irregular bloodied patch. The scalp and hair ripped out.

The rest of her hair is dropping bit by bit onto the sheet the nurse has placed around Chrissie's neck.

My clinical side kicks in.

The neuro arrives, we discuss it, I go and get Sam, the formalities are dealt with, consent signed, options and possible outcomes.

The reality?

Most of it's up to Chrissie.

We can only assist.

If there's anyone who's going to survive, it's her.

Chrissie has guts. At the end of the day the surgeons can only do so much. If you don't have the guts to fight, the best neuro in the world won't make an iota of difference.

I go with Sam out into the corridor.

Ellen has the practical suggestion we all get some dinner. It's well past Matthew's bedtime.

And they head out the hospital doors in search of food.

I stay at the hospital.

My Chrissie's a fighter. That's one thing we all agree on.

She'll never give up.

Never.

But now... we would have to wait.

The sound of an approaching ambulance siren, which fades until it is overridden by a heartbeat.

Lynette Anderson's story

Rhonda's next door neighbour.
Music: Dionne Warwick's 'That's what friends are for' or similar.

Lynette I never interfere in other people's business. What people do in the privacy of their own home is their own affair. As long as it doesn't affect me, fine. Each to his own.

Believe me, and I'm talking from first-hand experience here, once you start sticking your big nose into other people's affairs you're asking for trouble. Big time. Oh, no. Never go where you're not wanted. That's my motto.

However, there are exceptions.

And when it comes to Rhonda, well, she's practically blood.

And I've known Rhonda for donkey's years. We can practically read each other's thoughts.

What goes on behind her front door, remains behind that front door, likewise what goes on this side of the fence remains on this side of the fence.

But, and it's a big but, there is a line you've got to draw in any relationship.

Once that line's crossed, it's my belief, maybe not everybody else's, but my belief, you have an obligation to stick by your principles.

And I believe Graham over-stepped that line.

Rhonda's my friend.

God, it was a real moral dilemma for me. Do I tell her or don't I tell her? And if I do tell her, how much do I tell her?

Should I let sleeping dogs lie?

Maybe that's best.

Rhonda and Graham might sort it out themselves. They're adults after all. Don't need me to hold their hand.

But at the end of the day, well, Rhonda is my friend.

And, really, if I'm completely honest with myself, there really wasn't any question.

I had to have a good hard talking-to, myself.

'Lynette,' I said, 'Lynette, it's going to be torture, but you have to shoulder the responsibility. You have to tell Rhonda.'

I couldn't let Rhonda go on living in a fool's paradise. It just churned me up too much. And I hate hypocrites. Stand by your principles or what are your principles worth?

No, there was no choice. Not in this case.

And bottom line, you have to go back to that first question I asked myself: who else did Rhonda have to turn to?

You see, if the truth be known, Rhonda doesn't have many friends.

Most of Rhonda's friends that she has now started out as my friends. True. Rhonda got to know them through me, so they became Rhonda's friends as well.

She's such a quiet little thing usually. Wouldn't say boo to a mouse. So, who puts their hand up when the chips are down? Muggins here, of course.

But I do know where to draw the line, even if the boundaries are a bit blurred at times. I know when to pull back.

You know, when she and Graham first moved into that property there was an instant rapport between Rhonda and me.

From my kitchen you can practically see straight into Rhonda's.

Well, not straight in. But if you're standing on a chair reaching for something in one of my top cupboards, and you look over, you can see the top of Rhonda's head moving about her kitchen.

Not that I've got any time at all for people who just don't know when to keep out of things. There's a big question of privacy here.

But as soon as she and Graham moved in, Rhonda and I just clicked.

An instant bond.

Rhonda was forever beating a path down her front hall, out the door, down the pathway, into our garden—not that you could ever call our front

yard a garden, Dennis gives it so little attention—
and straight down the hall into my kitchen.

And this bond developed from there.

To be fair, I was just as guilty.

I'd get off the phone and have something I had to
tell her. Or be listening to the talkback on radio,
hear something I had to share, and I'd be off down
my passageway, out the front door, into Rhonda's
kitchen at the drop of a hat.

It was only inevitable that we put a gate in the
side fence.

It was practical, more than anything else.

You know, we'd be chatting, and Rhonda would
pour her heart out to me. I should have said
something back then.

Easy to be wise after the event.

Other times, we'd simply be having a discussion
about the economy, or international affairs. I like
to keep my finger on the pulse.

I'm not letting that university education go down
the gurgler.

Anyway, we'd be having a bit of a catch-up and
I'd hear my phone ring. Why people never call
the mobile, I'll never know. So off I'd dash, down
Rhonda's front hall, out the door, leap the fence,
into the front door, down my front passage and
the phone stops. I'm not giving Telstra any more
money using those numbers you call to get who
dialled last.

Oh, no. You have to get up a bit earlier to catch this worm.

So it was only a matter of time, inevitable really, that I got Dennis to put that gate in the side fence.

And in my opinion that gate added value to Rhonda and Graham's property.

Not that Rhonda and I live in each other's pockets.

God, I couldn't bear that. But there were times when she needed me. That's all I'll say on the matter.

Last week was definitely one of those times.

You see, I had an instinct something was up months ago. I'm a very intuitive person. I could tell.

It was no surprise when I saw Graham with this blonde bit leaving McDonald's.

Give him his due, he had moved out of the matrimonial home a couple of months previous. [*Making an inverted comma sign*] 'Trial separation'.

Well, Graham was definitely trying it and liking it that afternoon. No point in hiding it from Rhonda anymore.

He'd sworn blind that there was no one else involved. And there was the evidence staring me in the face.

The pair of them were slobbering all over each other like a couple of teenagers.

Finally, Graham withdraws his tongue—oh yes, it was wide screen and technicolour—he squeezes her backside, makes me sick to think about it, and she disappears into the cheap jewellery place at North Course Plaza. You know the type of place. Display window crammed with cheap gold bracelets and necklaces.

She obviously worked there.

Don't know what Graham was doing there at that time of day because he works clear across town. What cock and bull story his workplace was being strung is nobody's business.

Well, Rhonda took the news as expected.

Said nothing. Not a peep out of her.

I asked her if there was anything I could do. Pick up Damien from school? It was almost two-thirty. Thought she might like a couple of hours to herself. Digest things.

Not one little bit.

No.

Rhonda, grabs her raincoat, picks up the car keys, heads straight out the door.

Doesn't take an Einstein to guess where she was heading.

And what sort of friend would I be if I didn't go along for moral support?

Not for a moment, not in my wildest dreams did I believe Rhonda'd confront the woman.

Not the remotest possibility. That's just not Rhonda's style.

All I did was suggest she perhaps think things through a bit before she speaks to this woman.

We're weaving through mid-afternoon traffic all this while.

I'm offering support.

'Have it clear in your head what you want to do. Have it clear what you want to say. Don't go at it like a bull at a gate, for God's sake.'

You know, you've got a much better chance of achieving your objectives if you've thought things through, got a level head and approach the task in an objective, not subjective manner. I didn't do two years of university for nothing.

Well, all this was obviously going in one of Rhonda's ears and out the other.

She's barely acknowledging my presence in the car. But we find a park all right, Rhonda looks well in control of things.

All was fine 'til we start heading up the escalator and there's Donovan's Discount Jewellery store straight ahead.

Rhonda grabs my hand.

God, I thought my circulation was going to be cut off, she was holding it so tight.

Kept my calm, though.

All I said was, 'You all right?'

Rhonda nods.

Then we get to the top of the escalators and that's when I see her.

The blonde.

She's walking towards the store.

'That's her!' I said.

And that's all I said.

Honest to God.

That is all I said.

'That's her.'

I didn't say, 'Go introduce yourself'.

I didn't say, 'Go give her a piece of your mind'.

I didn't say, 'Go and tell her you know about her and Graham'.

Nothing like that.

All I said was, 'That's her'.

Well, Rhonda takes off like a shot out of a canon. This extraordinary sound coming out of her mouth.

It's a screaming, wailing sound like I've never heard in my life, and it doesn't stop. It rolls on and on out of her body.

A sea of people just part as Rhonda comes flying across the marble floor, her hands waving in the air and this peculiar screaming wailing sound filling the food court atrium.

And as Rhonda gets to the blonde woman she grabs her hair from behind and starts yanking it.

And she's yanking the hair and kicking her at the same time.

The two of them are going around and around and around in circles. This wailing screaming sound and Rhonda and the blonde.

Spinning around and around and around.

And nobody stopping them.

Everyone just staring at the blonde and Rhonda as they go around and around.

That's when I see, through the crowd, across the food court in front of the discount jewellery shop, this woman with a mobile phone. She's beckoning, waving at two security guards on the next level, then pointing to Rhonda and the blonde.

Oh God, this is going to be trouble. I can see it.

And that's when it struck me.

The blonde with the phone is the one who'd been with Graham, not the one with Rhonda.

Oh God! What is she doing? Rhonda's attacking the wrong woman! It's too awful for words. Rhonda's attacking a complete stranger.

Well, the security guards are still pushing their way down the escalator as Rhonda and the blonde spin toward the tables and chairs in the food court.

That's when I see it.

A half-melted kiddy's ice-cream cone lying on the marble floor.

Rhonda's foot steps into it, or the blonde's, I can't be too sure on that, but Rhonda is still making this awful, awful screaming wailing sound as the two of them go down like nine pins.

Then it's silence.

Everything and everyone stops.

The only sound in the entire atrium is the musak playing in the background, and this almighty crack, as the blonde's head hits the marble floor.

That's when security guards finally gets to Rhonda, a bit too late, but what do you expect, you pay peanuts you get monkeys?

The crowd's just standing around. Gawping.

And the blonde with the mobile, the one who's been the raison d'être for this entire incident, just disappears back into Donovan's Discount Jewellery.

Oblivious.

Completely oblivious to the mayhem she's causing.

Oh God, what has Rhonda done?

What has my dear, dear friend done?

Before I know it, there are sirens wailing and paramedics rushing in all directions. I couldn't get near Rhonda. She's slumped on a chair, clutching a handkerchief covered in blood.

Then the security people are carting her off. The blonde woman's being lifted onto the stretcher, and covered by a blanket. They took her straight to hospital.

I'm trying to get Dennis on the mobile all the while this chaos was happening around me.

When I finally get him and explain what's happened, Rhonda's well gone.

No one seemed to know exactly where.

The management were completely unhelpful.

So I head out to the carpark to wait for Dennis, who finally pulls up in the Range Rover as the cleaner's walking off with his mop and bucket of bloodied water.

I have got a migraine by this stage.

And I'm a complete cot case when I get a migraine.

People can be so irresponsible.

Imagine buying a child an ice-cream cone, then dropping it, and leaving it for someone to slip on.

Look at the chaos they've caused.

What effort does it take to pick up an ice-cream cone?

None at all.

And guess what? All that was left as evidence of this whole sorry episode, were a few witch's hats and a sign saying 'Beware Slippery Floor'.

No, you need to know when to draw a line.

I do.

Pity about Rhonda.

That awful screaming, wailing sound. It'll haunt me for years.

But I'll stick by her. After all, what are friends for?

However it's not up to me to tell her the woman's dead.

No. That's Graham's job.

After all, if it wasn't for Graham, none of this would have happened.

The lights fade.

The sound of ambulance and police sirens build.

They fade and a child's voice sings:
  'Row, row, row, your boat,
  Gently down the stream,
  When you see a crocodile,
  Don't forget to scream.
  Row, row, row, your boat…'

Matthew's story

Matthew McKinnon is aged four and a half.
He holds a cardboard shoebox in his hands. It has a lid. He also holds a toy truck. He pushes it along the floor, mimicking the ambulance siren as he does so.

Matthew 'Row, row, row your boat,
　　　　Gently down the stream,
　　　　When you see a crocodile,
　　　　Don't forget to scream.'

Hello. I've got a pet lizard.

And do you know what? My lizard doesn't have a tail. We don't know where it went.

You know what my lizard's name is? His name is Lilly.

My sister, her name is Ellen, she says I broke Lilly's tail off. But I didn't. It's not true. I didn't break Lilly's tail off. We don't know where Lilly's tail is. He never had a tail really.

And do you know what else? Lilly lives in this box. And he sleeps in my room with me.

But last night I slept in my mummy's bed. But my mummy wasn't there. Only Lilly and me.

And my dad wasn't there, too. No he wasn't.

He visits us, but he doesn't sleep with Mummy in her bed.

You know what? I sleep in my bed, and Ellen sleeps in her bed and Lilly sleeps in his box in my room, and Daddy sleeps in his place and Alex, she sleeps at our place too.

But, last night I slept in Mummy's bed.

And do you know what else? My mummy's having a party. And Alex said I could take Lilly to Mummy's party.

And do you know when Mummy's party is? It's this afternoon. And we're going to have a funelran first and then all the people are coming back to our place for the party for Mummy. And then Mummy will be back here. Because she hasn't been home for the last three days.

No. She hasn't.

And I've missed her a lot. No, Mummy's been getting ready for her funelran and the party. So I won't be able to sleep in Mummy's bed tonight with Alex, because Mummy will want her bed back, won't she?

And I'll take Lilly into my room, and Ellen will be in her room, and Daddy will be at his flat, and Mummy will be in her bed.

And do you know what else? Ellen said I was fucking stupid.

And I dobbed on her. I did. I dobbed on Ellen.

And do you know what Alex said? She said I wasn't stupid. So I told Ellen I wasn't stupid.

And Ellen said I broke Lilly's tail off and I was fucking stupid.

And I said, 'I'm not fucking stupid'.

And Ellen said, 'You are fucking stupid'.

And I said, 'I'm not'.

And Ellen said I'm fucking stupid because Mummy's not coming back.

And… and, I said, 'She is'.

And Ellen said, 'She's not'.

And I said, 'We're going to Mummy's funelran and she's having a party. And Alex said I'm allowed to take Lilly to the funelran. Alex said so.'

So I pushed Ellen.

I got a smack for that.

You're not allowed to push Ellen.

And do you know what else?

My daddy and Alex were yelling at one another.

My daddy said Alex shouldn't be in Mummy's bed.

But it's all right.

I was in there too. Mummy wouldn't mind. I don't wet my bed anymore. I'm four and a half. So it's all right, see?

Mummy wouldn't be angry with me.

And Daddy and Alex were still yelling.

And Mrs Carlisle from next door comes in and she says to come with her.

But I don't want to go with Mrs Carlisle.

She's got a big dog called Jodie. And I don't like Jodie. She barks at me through the fence.

[*Calling out*] Jodie!

Jodie is very big. Jodie! Jodie!

Jodie barks.

And do you know what else? I want to stay with Daddy. He might take me to his flat. Maybe that's where Mummy's staying 'til her funelran. But then Mrs Carlisle said she was making some sausage rolls for Mummy's party, and I love sausage rolls.

But I didn't really want to go with Mrs Carlisle because Jodie's next door.

Jodie! Jodie! I don't like Jodie. She barks at me through the fence. [*Calling out*] Woof! Woof! Jodie!

Jodie barks.

And I want my mummy back.

I don't want to stay with Mrs Carlisle this afternoon.

And Daddy's back at his place now.

And I don't know where Alex is.

And Ellen's playing at her friends.

And I want Mummy!

Do you know where my mummy is?

His bottom lip goes.

I want my mummy! I want my mummy.
And I'm not stupid.
And I didn't break off Lilly's tail.
Where's my mummy? I want my mummy!
I want my mummy!

Matthew lifts the lid and looks in the box.

It will be all right, won't it, Lilly?
I love Lilly. Even if he hasn't got a tail.

Matthew replaces the lid.

We're going to my mummy's party.
You want to come?
Go on! I'll save you a sausage roll.

He smiles.

The lights fade.

END ACT ONE

ACT TWO

Graham Russell's story

A pub at meal time.
A finger taps on a live mike.

Voice-over Testing… testing. [*They blow into the mike.*] Testing.

Feedback.

Testing… Could I have your attention.

Patrons note that due to an industrial dispute, there's no table service tonight. Order your meals at the bar and we'll give you a numbered ticket.

Loud feedback.

Jeez!

Number 72 and75. 72 and 75, your meal's ready. And 61, bolognese and chips, whoever ordered the bolognese and chips they've been sitting here for fifteen minutes…'

Graham Russell, a developing beer gut, wearing a suit, a beer in one hand, a numbered ticket in the other, enters.

He urinates against the back wall, before zipping up, taking a quick gulp before holding forth.

Graham Lynette? How can I describe Lynette. Like having a zit you know you shouldn't squeeze, because it'll keep coming back, and back. Well, that's what it was like with me and Lynette.

Now Rhonda, she's my boy Damien's mother, well Rhonda had barely been in the clink six months before it all started.

I mean I'd given Lynette a quick shag up against the back fence one night during a party. But that was all. Nothing more to it than that.

A quick shag, wipe it down, whack it back in, pour yourself a beer, party goes on, go home with the missus.

It was her old man Dennis's birthday. We were both pissed. So what? Nothing came of it.

Oh no, hang on, I lie. The score sheet doesn't necessarily tell all the facts.

Amazing thing about statistics, you can make 'em read almost any way you want.

Case in point. Lynette did give me a blow job. Once. Under the cumquat tree by the dog kennel. But that doesn't really count. Doesn't count 'officially'. And that's historical fact. Remember Clinton?

No, the true score on the tally board with Lynette was one quick shag up against the back fence during me mate Dennis's fortieth. Harmless. A bit of neighbourly skylarking.

Well, not six months later Rhonda's residing at Her Majesty's Pleasure, Lynette and I are doing it on the kitchen table, we're doing it in the bathroom, out on the barbie, in the car, hanging from the rafters in the garage. I've never know a brunette to go off like that.

As for Rhonda. God that was a bloody awful business.

Who knows what was going through her head when she attacked that woman.

And people wonder why I'd moved out of the matrimonial home?

There's one good reason why.

That person could've been me.

I could've been lying six foot under now instead of that poor cow at the shopping mall.

That could've been Graham Russell with a bloody axe through his skull or worse. No kidding mate, that could've been me.

And, to add insult to injury, Tanya, she was the blonde I was officially with at the time, well she puts two and two together and gets ten. True.

Tanya, the little blonde Ruski thinks that because my ex has had a spazz attack and bumped someone off, that I could do the same thing.

I ask you? Where's the friggin' logic in that?

Nah, Rhonda doing in that woman at the shopping mall definitely put the kybosh on Tanya and my relationship.

Voice-over Ticket number 79 and 81. 79 and 81 ready to collect. No table service tonight due to Elaine throwing a hissy fit. And there's a bolognese and chips going begging. Number 61. 61.

Graham Tanya, jeeez, mate. Where do I start with Tanya?

That woman. Holy moly! That woman. Ooooh mate. It was like fucking a can of worms. I kid you not mate. A can of wriggly worms. Bloody fantastic.

There were drawbacks though.

You know what the real problem was with Tanya?

She wouldn't bloodywell commit.

You understand where I'm coming from?

I almost, I kid you not, I almost went to see a psych over Tanya.

Jeez that was a close call.

One day at work I wasn't focussing, hadn't been for weeks.

Graham Russell was on a downward spiral, oblivion staring him in the face.

Had to grab myself by the scruff of the neck and say, 'Graham, Gra, get yourself to the quack'.

Well I went down to the works' quack. About a hundred yards down the road, where we get our annual flu shot.

Not a bad sort. I'd give her one. Anyway, she reckons I was in such a bad state, drugs wouldn't fix it. I should see a shrink.

No way. No fucking way mate.

Graham Russell is stronger than that.

Graham Russell wasn't team leader, then section manager, then divisional manager all in the space of two years because he couldn't sort out his own fucking problems.

No way matey.

I'd moved out of the family nest, hadn't I?

I'd set up a nice little bachelor pad. Too right.

I could sort out my own problems.

But before I even have a chance to prioritise, the shit hits the fan with Rhonda.

No question then, no choice either.

Rhonda's in the slammer, so I have to move back into the family abode.

Lost the bond on the townhouse for that!

Thank you very much Rhonda.

But, and this is the real tragedy, the glorious blonde Tanya has got me by the balls. And I mean she's got 'em mate. In the palm of her hand! Didn't know whether I was coming or going.

I'm trying to wrestle bloody work commitments, me boy Damien's acting all peculiar, and God knows what else, and then, just to complicate things, suddenly Lynette from next door is popping through that bloody side gate.

'You in Grah? You there? Got a spare bit of beef curry.'

Curry isn't the bloody half of it.

Those knickers were off quicker than a prawn in a heatwave. As I said, in the kitchen, on the barbie, hanging from the rafters. Whoo!

It was all over red rover for Tanya and me.

I mean, with shagging Lynette all day, there was very little sauce left in the bottle for Tanya at night. Practically bone dry.

And she was getting pissed mate. Really pissed.

You ever seen a pissed Russian? Not attractive. Doesn't hold back mate. Yabber, yabber, yabber. Didn't understand half of it, but I got the meaning all right.

Truth be known, I saw a really ugly side to Tanya that I'd never witnessed before.

And as a very good mate of mine had warned me already, 'Grah, a word from the wise. Before you commit, get a look at her mother.'

And you know why? Because that's what that hot bit of Ruski is going to look like in twenty years time.

Well mate, lucky I did. Lucky I did.

Next time I'm at Tanya's place I spy a king-size portrait of this heifer back in Mother Russia.

Tanya's old lady.

Strewth, you can be lucky. Lucky escape, very lucky escape mate.

So that's the end of Tanya and me.

But now, Lynette's demanding more! And more and more. And I'm beginning to feel a bit guilty about Dennis.

He is my mate after all.

And truth be known, if you do shag your mate's missus, to my way of thinking anyway, it can only be a one-off event.

Honest to God, I really believe this.

It's not something that you can do on an ongoing basis.

I mean, where are your principles?

It's just not acceptable behaviour.

So something had to be done on that front. And pronto.

And of course there was bloody Rhonda.

Let's not forget Rhonda. Jeez.

I started getting these begging letters from the clink. Can you believe it?

Bad enough everyone had to know that Rhonda was doing time, did she ever think of what me and Damien are going through? Nah. Not once.

What that boy had to put up with at school is nobody's business.

It was on the tele, in the papers, hard to keep my head up at work, and now Rhonda was writing begging letters.

That's what really started to do my head in.

'Please visit.' 'Please bring our son.' 'Please call.' What did she think I was? I'm not her bloody support network.

There was a definite trial separation in progress when Rhonda lost the plot.

Where's Bruce and Eileen's part in all this? They're her parents after all.

They may be a bit long in the tooth, and live across the other side of town, but there's always public transport isn't there? Oh yes.

Can't use lack of a car as an excuse for not visiting their only daughter.

Doesn't wash with me.

'Get on a train you lazy old bastards.'

God I was quick to catch on to those two codgers.

'My taxes go to pay for your daughter's stay in the clink!

'My taxes go to give you your pension.

'And what's more, I get taxed so you two bastards can get a bloody pensioner discount on public transport. I'm not giving you any more.'

Oh yes, I was a wake-up to Bruce and Eileen.

And don't ask me to travel all the way out to Woop Woop on my day off. It's just not on.

Truth be known mate, my life was turning into hell.

Promotion?

Jeez, I was lucky to keep my job.

Suddenly I'm seeing people I started with, blokes who I'd previously left in the starting blocks, get promotion over me.

I'm seeing these nice enough blokes, but hardly promotion material, getting fast-tracked, and me shunted sideways. What is going on?

Rhonda, that's what.

Rhonda was all over the television. No hope of keeping it quiet. Not a hope in hell.

That's when Lynette of all people, Lynette who knew all the facts, was there at the start, well Lynette starts putting the hard word on me too.

She wants to move in. Permanent. Well, what can I say? She's an adult. I can't make up her mind for her.

Damien's starting to get ratty. Dennis is threatening to deck me. Me? Jesus, what have I done?

'Dennis, will you shut up for one second and listen to a bit of reason? I'm not the one who wants to fly the coop. You're the one who needs to sort it out with Lynette mate. Not me. So don't go threatening me. You sort out your own problems.'

Shut him up all right.

Well, couple of months after that, Lynette's tossed her lot in here with me, and it's full-on.

Yep, from that moment, it was on for young and old.

Dennis's bolted the gate.

Well, that's that friendship down the plug hole.

No more neighbourly barbies. No more beers on a summer's night. Definite frosty reception on that front.

Damien's gone to live with his gran and pop. Well Eileen and Bruce, see if you can handle a teenage boy going through puberty?

Oh yes, think you can do a better job? Go for it.

As for Dennis, well, can't blame him can you?

Not really.

When I look at it dispassionately, well, I was shaggin' his wife after all.

Mind you Dennis is no saint. But I personally am not one to tell tales out of school. Not my style.

However, if things ever got nasty, if ever Dennis wants to get legal, well, I've definitely got the dirt on Dennis.

As for Rhonda and those letters?

Well, I kept well clear of the trial.

Rhonda's old enough to look after herself. I've got enough on my plate.

And truth be known, it's nothing to do with me, so why should I go?

Who's looking after the home front?

Me, that's who.

The sentence? A stiff one, but stiff cheddar.

Twelve years. Non-parole period of nine.

Beers all round?

The noise of the pub swells as the lights fade.

Voice-over Number 97, and 95. Your dinner's ready. And number 61. Number 61 has just been listed with the National Trust!

The end of an evening radio traffic report.

Radio voice It's bumper to bumper on the Northern Expressway, give that a big miss. Estimated time from the city to the North Causeway exit, twenty minutes, traffic flowing pretty well once you get off. If you're heading south, there's a three-car pile-up on the South Eastern, so try and avoid that if you can, and the boys in the 'Eye in the Sky' say all lanes leading west out along the ring road are at a standstill. A truck's lost its load...

Static as the station is changed.

Radio voice And in other parts of the world, Rome 16, Paris 15 degrees and wet, London a mild 17 degrees, New York 14, Chicago a chilly 6...

Static as the station is changed.

Radio voice … and that's all from the news team. If you're looking for relief from the heat and heading to the beach, don't forget to 'slip, slop, slap'. Now it's back to Lobby and the Breakfast Crew…'

Static as the station is changed.

Radio voice … and this morning's topic on the open line: 'Should the Shahir family be allowed to stay or should the Minister give them the old heave-ho?' You know what I think, let's hear your comments…

Mrs Joan Carlisle's story

Mrs Carlisle sits on her front porch in a long dressing gown. She turns off her transistor radio, then looks to the sky to verify the weather. She takes a lemon acid drop from a tin she holds and puts it in her mouth.

Joan You know, if you suck it gently, you can make a McIllwraith's Acid Drop last almost all day long.

You used to be able to buy them loose. At Perc Hennessy's sub-newsagency.

Up on the corner of Waltham Parade and George Street. He's the only sub-newsagent still operating now.

There used to be one on almost every corner.

Big Peter's ice-cream cone that lit up at night. And a sign on the door 'Hennessy's Now Open', or if you turned it around, 'Sorry Closed'. Really smart operators like Perc Hennessy, well, he had a written notice on the counter too. In his own beautiful copperplate handwriting.

'Stamps sold here'. I'm not certain it was completely legal, but it was a service to the neighbourhood. Used to be able to get a stamp on a Sunday. Not anymore.

When they stopped selling McIllwraith's Acid Drops loose, and that would've been, oh well over thirty years ago now, Perc Hennessy got them in especially for me.

In these little tins.

Which are very handy, because when you want a break, you can just take them out of your mouth, and pop them on the lid.

Mrs Carlisle takes the acid drop out of her mouth and places it on the tin lid.

You don't lose any of the flavour doing this, and as long as you keep an eye out, and shoo the blowies away, it even enhances the taste.

And it makes them last longer, too.

Almost to the end of the day.

In fact, I've woken up in the morning to find that I've still got one from yesterday sitting on the lid on my bedside table. Next to my teeth.

And whenever I buy my tin of McIllwraith's Acid Drops from Perc Hennessy, he gives me any magazines he can't sell. Not out of charity though. It's because they're ripped or otherwise damaged and he can't sell them.

She unrolls a magazine she holds.

Keeps me in touch. He's one of a dying breed, Perc Hennessy.

She pops the acid drop back in her mouth.

I'm waiting for the nurse. She gives me a shower every Monday, Wednesday and Friday. It's a raffle who you get, let alone when they will turn up.

Isn't it Jodie, eh?

Poor Jodie. She's got very bad arthritis in her hips.

She acknowledges a passer-by.

Morning.

Jodie barks.

Down Jodie, down.

She won't bite. She's harmless really.

Come here, that's a girl. You sit down and rest that bad hip of yours.

You sit here long enough you'll see the world go by.

She takes the acid drop out of her mouth, places it on the tin lid, and opens the magazine.

Now what's Fergie been up to this week? Oh.

Morning Ellen.

Jodie barks.

Down Jodie, down. You leave Ellen alone Jodie. Off to uni are you? That's nice, you look very smart. I'm waiting for the girl from the council. For my shower. 'Bye, dear, enjoy your day.

Ellen's a lovely girl. Alex has done a sterling job bringing up that child. Almost single-handedly. And Ellen as a kiddy was a handful. What would I have done in that situation? Doesn't bear thinking about.

Matty? Altogether different really. He was such a lovely little boy. Wasn't he Jodie? We loved Matty when he was a little boy, didn't we? Wish we could say the same thing about him now.

It was the in-vitro fertilisation. That's what I believe. A test-tube baby, and look what he turned out like.

I can still see that sweet little face standing at my front door. A mass of red curls under his baseball cap.

Loved my butterfly cakes. Couldn't get enough of my sausage rolls.

Yet as he got older, this very, very nasty streak started to develop.

I first noticed it when I found him out on the nature strip one day.

I was on my way to the butcher's to get some lambs' hearts for Jodie.

There used to be three butchers' shops in High Street, now there's none. You could get half a dozen lambs' hearts and a few shanks for less than a dollar. Last us all week, wouldn't it Jodie?

Now I've got to go all the way over to Woolworths.

She checks her watch.

If that woman's not here by now, I know it'll be well after ten before I have a shower.

Anyway where was I? Oh yes, I was on my way to the butcher's that morning. It was autumn. A lovely time of year. Bit of a nip in the air, but glorious sunshine.

There was little Matthew out on the nature strip.

He had his pet lizard he kept in a box. Took the thing everywhere.

Don't know if it was the same one or not.

It was only a skink, Christine might've replaced it once a week.

How long does a skink live?

That's an interesting question.

Who knows?

Doesn't matter really, but Matty used to keep it in a cardboard box.

He was out on the nature strip this morning and the cardboard box was on the ground.

I said, 'Is that your lizard's house, Matty?'

And he just muttered something like, 'Mrs Carlisle, you know what?'. He had a habit of prefacing everything he said with, 'You know what?'. It was a way of speaking that invited you to converse. A very endearing trait in one so young.

'Do you know what Mrs Carlisle?'

'What Matty?', I said

And he said, 'I don't want Lizzy anymore'.

I think that's what he used to call it, Lizzy the lizard?

And I said something like, 'Oh, Matthew, poor Lizzy. That's not a very nice thing to say.'

Well, he turned around, virtually spat the words out at me.

'I hate Lizzy.'

And he trod on the box. And the language!

Well I just ignored the boy. Headed off to the butcher's.

But on my way back, outside his house, on the nature strip where he'd been playing, there was a small pile of ashes.

Can you believe it? He'd burnt the little lizard in its box.

What a cruel thing to do to an innocent.

All these years later things haven't improved.

From such a sweet little boy he's unfortunately grown into a very nasty young man. The police have been around once. A knife was involved I believe. Graffiti on the railway carriage another time. Got off with a warning. Alex has got her hands full with Matthew.

Perhaps he'll grow out of it, eh Jodie?

Eleven is a difficult age. He's not a boy, he's not a teenager.

He misses his mother, but, you do have to ask yourself how much of his mother he remembers?

He was only four and a half at the time after all.

Ellen was the one I felt for.

The buckets of tears that girl shed. Still makes me upset even to think about it now, all these years later.

Alex had to physically hold her up at the funeral.

I've never, ever seen anything like that in my life.

Ellen grieved and grieved until I thought, well, she will never get over the loss of her mother. That's it. This is her lot in life.

Some people don't.

You can't put a time limit on grief. Don't believe a word anyone says to the contrary.

When I lost my husband of forty-two years, Arthur, Arthur Gordon Carlisle was his full name, well my life stopped.

Our life as I had known it for forty-two years was over.

God hadn't blessed Arthur and me with children so there was no comfort there.

And I'm the youngest of seven.

All gone.

You know, people say that these are the best years of your life?

I'd like to hit them.

I'm sure Matty's problems are all tied up with losing his mother. And the IVF.

You come out of a test tube, what can you expect?

> *Mrs Carlisle pops the acid drop back in her mouth and sucks on it for a moment, surveying the street. She then reads from an article.*

'Nicole's tears—heartbreak changed my life.' Hmmm…

Christine's case was in here.

Oh yes, Christine's case was headline material for quite some time.

Made into quite a number of the magazines Perc gave me.

Big articles too.

A neighbour of the woman who'd killed Christine figured very prominently.

A rather cheap-looking brunette. Very c.o.m.m.o.n.

This brunette had fallen 'in love'. She'd fallen passionately in love with the murderer's husband.

'Love'?

Silly cow didn't look as if she knew the meaning of the word.

Dumped her own husband, and moved in with the chap next door.

The one whose wife was in prison.

I cut out that article. It's inside somewhere.

Oh yes, it was headline material for quite some time.

Headline material. Then forgotten.

I have great admiration for the way Alex Doucette handled the whole business.

It wasn't easy for anyone. But especially for Alex.

She has such… such grace.

And intelligence.

I admire Alex Doucette enormously.

Very well-regarded in the medical world apparently.

However, we're not much enamoured with her new 'friend'.

Claire. Bit full of herself, Claire.

And bossy.

Still, if Alex likes her, and Ellen gets on with her, we'll give her the benefit of the doubt, eh Jodie?

What I still can't come to terms with though, and to my way of thinking this is the most confounding and upsetting aspect of the whole business, is Ellen's campaign for the woman's release from prison. Just doesn't sit with me.

She's a very bright cookie Ellen.

But I can't understand that.

Call me old-fashioned, but I wouldn't want that woman back on the streets, I'd want her dead.

She takes the acid drop out of her mouth.

Oh, look Jodie, no rest for the wicked. Here's trouble.

Jodie barks. Mrs Carlisle stands.

Come on in love. She won't bite. She's harmless really. Down Jodie. Get off the lady. She's harmless. She won't bite. She's like me, hasn't got any teeth. Down Jodie! Down!

Mrs Carlisle hurls the magazine in the direction of Jodie.

Down.

First, a large pink morning coat is thrown over her shoulders.

Down.

Next the head comes back and it is a mass of long blonde curls.

Voice-over Down they go. Crazy, never-to-be-repeated prices. Nine-carat gold pendants were $49.99 slashed to $35.99. Pure silver lockets were $89.99, now a crazy $59.99.

Genuine nine-carat gold bracelets with eternity heart locket was $79.99, now a crazy $39.99. The heart-shaped locket alone would be worth $39.99, but today we are throwing them away. Lovely things. Unbelievable prices.

Donovan's end-of-lease sale, so everything is marked down.

Down! Down! Down! Donovan's prices are down!

Repeat if necessary.

Tanya's story

Tanya Moisevitch, 38, proprietor of Donovan's Discount Jewellery, sits at her dressing table.

Tanya Down, down, down it went.

She applies cold cream to her face.

Right down Tanya's throat.

This is Graham Russell's tongue I speak with you.

Graham Russell's tongue? Right down my throat!

What I say to make him do this to me?

Me, Tanya Moisevitch from Minsk.

You know, is old family joke: 'Tanya, the "Minx from Minsk"'.

Good joke, no? And there is some truth in this.

Tanya knows what is what. Okay?

But for me is always business first.

As for this Graham Russell, no, no, definitely no.

She continues with her ablutions.

You know with this one, when I first see him, I think, 'So what?'

Big meathead.

Not interest me at all.

But sometimes you have to get involved with these guys for business.

All I want is business, when all they are thinking of is bed.

Same all the world over.

Even in Minsk.

My family, for many, many years have jewellery in Minsk. Now here also. Four stores already.

Donovan's Discount Jewellery.

Why Donovan's? Is good question, but don't ask.

That is where I meet this Graham Russell.

I don't understand what I give him that he think I like him?

You know, it was not anything from me.

He come into the shop.

Always hanging around the shop.

Sometimes he buys, sometimes not.

We make small talk. Lah-de-dah. Nothing more. Nothing!

Well, I'm buying a hamburger for lunch one day, and he's behind me in the queue.

He offer to pay.

Like little boy. But sweet.

'Oh, thank you Graham.'

That it. Nothing more.

'Thank you Graham.'

You know, hamburger, big deal. Next time I'll order fries too.

So, I finish eating, get up to leave, and Graham, last of big spenders, grab me.

This I kid you not.

The meathead grabs me on the backside.

Both hands clamped hard on my backside.

I am so shocked I open my mouth.

And Graham meathead Russell pushes his face into mine and sticks his tongue down my throat. Yuck!

His grip's so strong, and the filthy bastard is getting a hard-on!

Bang in middle of food court!

Hundreds of people looking.

Children around.

God, what is happening? What is this man?

He buy hamburger, now this?

Finally Graham lets go and he says, 'I love you, Tanya'.

What?!

This man's been in my shop maybe half a dozen times.

Seen my family photo on counter.

Small talk, weather, football, lah-de-dah.

What the hell is this man talking about? Love?

Lust is for this one. No love.

Well, I pull myself together. 'Oh, Graham, I am touched you like me.'

But he is staring.

Mouth hard.

I don't want this one in the shop no more. Definite not in the shop!

I say, 'I am touched you have these feelings, but I don't feel the same way. Goodbye Graham.'

That it.

Definite end of story.

Then, one day Tanya hear Graham Russell's wife is a 'killer'.

A murderess.

Now, now it all make sense to me.

Finally, all pieces fit together.

Mr Graham meathead's wife is a killer, so he looked for love with Tanya.

What can I say?

Look elsewhere meathead!

Tanya not interest.

Not interest, and never will be.

Sad, but is life.

She pulls off her blonde wig.

Nothing is what it seems.

Tanya laughs. She turns her back to the audience.

Music.

Rhonda at fifty-three

A door slams—metal on metal.
The rattle of keys. The keys turn in a lock as a prison
door opens then shuts.
Rhonda Russell pulls the sheet off the clothes line,
folds it.
She stands in the morning sun, in her prison outfit.

Rhonda Time.

That's what I've got plenty of.

Reflection.

That's how I spend my time.

My time.

Not the time I spend working.

Or the time I'm on duty in the kitchen.

Or the time I'm working in the grounds.

Not the time I spend re-educating myself.

But that window of time I call my own.

It's a present.

I receive it every day.

This gift of time is private.

It's what I live for.

It's private.

It's my communion.

In seven hundred and sixty-eight days, time will be mine again.

Have I wasted time?

On reflection, yes.

That would have to be the honest answer.

So much of it was wasted.

Now though, I have educated myself in the management of time.

There is the time before my education, and there is the time after. And for me those two worlds are now very clearly defined.

If you had asked me to define naive beforehand, I would have pointed to a small child. I would never have thought of turning the finger and aiming it at myself.

I was a woman of mature years after all.

Innocence is the province of the very young and very old, but naive can span a lifetime.

When I first stepped into this world, two thousand nine hundred and eighty-four days ago, innocence took on a completely new meaning.

Instance.

The librarian. Been to a top private school.

The intelligence of high achiever.

'Rhonda, I didn't do it.'

Naive believed.

Never doubted it.

Later, when the librarian had time back in her control, she was being interviewed on the radio about an exhibition of paintings.

A glorious success.

I felt emotions I hadn't felt for years.

Until the interviewer asked the question.

'Can you tell me, now that you're out. Did you do it?'

And the answer? 'Yes.'

You fraud!

You lying fraud!

Oh yes, education is a glorious thing, but it can't alleviate naivety.

Only experience can do that.

Graham's never been to visit.

Did I expect him to?

Yes.

Was I disappointed when he didn't?

For the first four hundred and seven days, yes.

After that, no.

Experience.

Lynette was coming. Once. But she got lost.

Never tried coming again.

72

Lost.

Oh yes.

There's a story there all right.

Not that I care much anymore.

Waste of time.

Mum bought Damien over when he wasn't old enough to come by himself.

Now he's old enough, he pops in occasionally.

I don't expect any more. Naive to even think otherwise.

I'm thankful Damien pops in at Christmas. There will be time for more.

He's very quiet on certain subjects.

His father, Graham, for one.

And Lynette.

Don't know what you'd call her?

Ex-neighbour. De-facto stepmother?

Just about fills the bill.

Damien's face was a picture when I first asked how things were on the home front.

I'd finally wheedled the truth out of him after Mum filled me in.

Damien's a hopeless liar. So transparent. Can see straight through him.

'Oh she's not too bad I suppose.'

Mum was more forthright.

'She's a tarty bitch Rhonda.'

I tried being a tad more diplomatic.

Damien did have to live under the same roof with Lynette after all, but Mum wouldn't have a bar of it.

'No Rhonda, you can say what you like, but I haven't got any time for that woman. She's a tarty bitch and a slut to boot.'

Graham and Lynette.

Well it only lasted, well, less than three hundred and sixty-five days.

Sometimes I wonder whose life is more of a mess, Graham and Lynette's or mine.

The most important thing to me is that Damien survives.

And on that front things don't look too bad. Not too bad at all.

And then there is Ellen.

An extraordinary girl.

She comes here, once a month. Regular as clockwork. She's been campaigning for my release since her fourteenth birthday.

That's when she first visited.

An extraordinary moment for me.

Defining.

I killed Ellen's mother, and Ellen visited me on her birthday.

When the request first came through, I told them I'd have to think about this.

But, after two days of weighing the pros and cons, it suddenly dawned on me that this was a fourteen-year-old girl I was talking about.

If a fourteen-year-old girl is bold enough, confident enough and ready to face me, then I had no right not to be equally as ready, and accept her invitation.

God I was nervous.

Ellen must have been, too. But it didn't show.

She has such maturity for one so young, even back then.

That day, when I came into the games room for the meeting, she was already there.

The room gets the full glare of the afternoon sun, and I had to squint at first to see her.

But there was no missing her.

This attractive, well-groomed, young woman, sitting calmly by the window, in the sun.

Jeans, pink top, pink sneakers, sunglasses.

As I approached Ellen held out her hand.

I apologised immediately.

'I'm sorry but no contact is permissible.'

Thought I'd jump in quickly before my supervisor opened her mouth.

'But how do you do Ellen,' I continued.

Sounded like a bloody school marm.

'But how do you do?'

Where did that come from?

And I sat down opposite her. Words flying out of my mouth in all directions.

I'd rehearsed this moment over and over, and now the time was here and I was talking non-stop garbage.

Until finally I blurted out.

'Why are you here?'

From my point of view you could have cut the air with a knife.

But Ellen reached over, and took my hand.

I turned to my supervisor, immediately said, 'Back off please. You can of course listen, but oblige the girl. Please.'

And the supervisor stepped away.

Ellen still held my hand and said, 'I'm a woman now'.

This is a fourteen-year-old girl I'm talking about, but she was spot-on. She wasn't a teenager. No.

Then she said, 'I don't have a mother, and there's no point in keeping hate bottled up inside for a person I don't know. So for my fourteenth birthday I made a pact with myself.'

Forthright, but controlled. That's the way she spoke.

A very even tone to her voice.

'As one of the steps towards my growing up, I thought I should meet you Mrs Russell. Disperse that hate. So here I am.'

And she smiled, 'It's my gift to me'.

My thoughts were tumbling over one another, trying to catch up.

Ellen hated me, and that's not too strong a word, she hated me, yet she was here.

Ellen was holding my hand, even though contact was forbidden. I knew I had to step up a level to meet this head-on.

And we did.

We carried on talking for the next hour.

And towards the end of that first visit we even laughed.

It is impossible to build bridges in an afternoon, and I don't know if that was her ultimate intention, presumptive of me to even think it.

But something had begun, and I felt privileged.

Then the visit was almost over.

'It's your birthday Ellen,' I said. 'I wish I had something to give you'.

Ellen brushed the notion aside.

'This is the gift. Goodbye.'

And she gets up to leave.

Suddenly this person who'd been sitting on the other side of the room comes over.

The room had several visitors groups dotted around. I hadn't noticed this woman before.

She takes Ellen's hand and begins to lead her to the door. Leading her.

Oh God.

The woman was not just holding her hand, she was guiding Ellen to the door.

We had been sitting in the sun. Ellen had sunglasses. I was so nervous, so preoccupied, I'd thought nothing of it.

And then the woman guiding Ellen to the door, turns to me and says, 'Hello Mrs Russell, I'm Alex Doucette. Thank you for giving your time to speak with Ellen. Good afternoon.'

And she leads Ellen out the door.

The sun in her eyes.

All that time, the sun was in her eyes.

I sat, where I'm sitting now, and will continue to sit so many times during my remaining days in this world. Getting to know this young woman. Amazed by her strength.

Daunted by the fact that very little if anything seemed to be an obstacle for her.

But above all, privileged to be allowed into her world.

Time for me is still measured in days to freedom.

But with each visit, my understanding of this young woman and her parent grows, and my understanding of freedom becomes clearer.

Ellen reveals a clarity of vision, even though she can't see.

And my time, the gift of time I had kept to myself, I now find I can share.

Not only with her.

She has taught me, shown me direction.

And given me the ultimate gift.

Ellen has given me the key to freedom.

From now on, I no longer have to sit in the sun to heal the wounds.

Rhonda takes a handkerchief from her pocket.

She unfolds it to reveal the old brown bloodstain. She holds it up to the light.

She sits back in the chair and covers her face with the handkerchief, protecting herself from the heat of the sun.

The lights fade.

THE END

www.currency.com.au

Visit Currency Press' new website now:

● Buy your books online

● Browse through our full list of titles, from plays to screenplays, books on theatre, film and music, and more

● Choose a play for your school or amateur performance group by cast size and gender

● Obtain information about performance rights

● Find out about theatre productions and other performing arts news across Australia

● For students, read our study guides

● For teachers, access syllabus and other relevant information

● Sign up for our email newsletter

The performing arts publisher